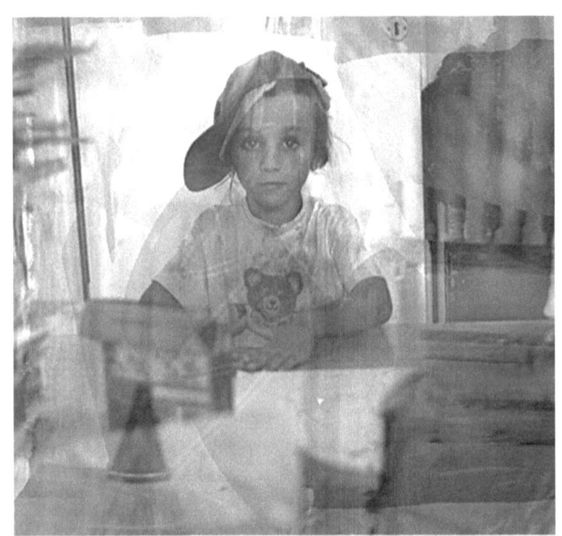

Art by Jadina Lilien

The Perfect Life

And Other Stories

Abel Wright

The Perfect Life and Other Stories by Abel Wright
Published by Stain'd Arts
Denver, CO 80206

www.staindmagazine.com

Cover by Noah Kaplan and Jadina Lillien.
Back Cover by Jadina Lillien.

ISBN: 978-1-948850-02-5

Contents

Preface

I write this to you inside a shortbread cookie container in a dimly lit room on a Saturday night at 10:51 pm. There are a fair number of things going on in this, a very nice and acommodable room. There is a lamp. A fan. A window that looks out at some grass. Sometimes if you're lucky you can see the skunk that lives in our backyard. I used to see the mama especially well when I was taking a shower in the early morning and the little waddling lady was taking herself to sleep and I'm just waking up and it's hot and steaming out the open window at eye level and she looks so sweet in all that hot water and yes — with a wall there between us. There are other things outside the window too. The telephone pole, wow, it's something, and all the old telephone wires that don't do much, and we have some lights hanging from the garage. And then your head just kind of falls, heads eventually fall, and you see all those books there, on the ground, next to the bed.

Carl Sagan called writing the greatest human invention. To have Dickinson, Emerson, Aurelius, and they just sleep right there next to me, whispering across the centuries. What a marvel, to be able to have done that, to put all one can imagine on to a page and give it away.

This collection of stories I would like to bill as fiction, though some of you may (indeed I hope many of you do) find things you recognize. I have made ample use of our lives. Me and yous. And not just my family yous, I also mean the you yous. Friends, roommates, brothers, love makers and other people, people I don't even know, people playing music in the park, people building furniture in their garages, people falling in love, people being polite, people going to poetry readings, getting upset, fighting. People eating ice cream and going for walks, holding babies and drinking whiskey. Both those sitting on a porch watching the moths fly around the streetlights thinking how beautiful it is and those that think—why do they do that, bash their heads against the light like that—what could they possibly be hoping for?

This is undoubtedly a questionable publishing of an otherwise admirable fingerpainting, which, though troubled, would, I imagine, make the refrigerator door. Although at times unbearably precious, for the reader sitting comfortably on their backside, or on their stomach in the grass, or curled up in bed with the lamp there—to the beloved and hungry reader, there is something to eat here. And if you do find yourself in any one of these positions, you may just see the shadow, the ghosts of a family— a mother and father, a sister, a baby, and a boy.

Lay on, stalwart reader.

Then, let us just say for now that these stories are for the ones who helped me write them, the ones who helped me be someone who would— for carolin, for mom, for dad, for murphy, jadina, and anyone I ever lived with, and for of course sweet Delia who I so believe in. And poetically
(I can't promise it is the end of it)

For the moon and for the moth.

1. The Perfect Life

He hugged his sister in the womb and knew he was not alone. She, who was more eager to see what, if anything, was making so much goddamn noise out there, slipped from his weightless embrace and into her beginning, leaving the boy to his thoughts. The boy did not fight this. He—who had so much to think about—sucked his thumb in the warm darkness of the womb discovering the pleasure of his own company. Being this close to god had its benefits, too, and he had no interest in leaving.

"They're going to have to come in here and get me, those crazy bastards. I see what's going on out there, don't think that I don't see," he said, to no one in particular.

The boy had everything but time. He was not yet sick with that particular affliction. Weak arms, though, he had in spades. Big nose, big ears—he would be a strangely proportioned child in the beginning. He was all eyes and would be unable to support his own head for far longer than was really reasonable or, to speak to closed-door sentiments, acceptable (his parents would worry, the neighbors would gossip, grow cruelly impatient). The weight of his reality would be heavy, unsteady, and often hard to control. He would learn to carry it, but it would take time.

He knew (the boy was brilliant in this way, and only nine months since his conception, it was just remarkable) that there was going to be a lot of shit to deal with out there. All the things outside his control—all the hate and fear—and really, he might quite tragically suffer too with the things he did not understand about how big and small he was, how easily broken and all he could do, how nature would manifest nightmares and dreams in his knees, all the things he would eat, how powerful and intricate and delicate he was. He was made of stardust, of light and air and dirt—asymmetrical and beautiful and he knew it. His time a blind act of balance and breadth, of food and oil. His skin shed away where he went, trying to contain him in the movement and stillness of his heart. It would be such a wild, exhilarating thing—but ultimately an exhausting experience he just assumed put off for some time. He liked the silence.

His birth was painful, as births tend to be. The boy would not forget that. Just as well, he would have reminders of it throughout his life that he would treasure like the places inside him that most resembled god (somewhere inside of you too), knowing that pain was an important thing to feel in this perfect life. He knew it would make his bowl bigger, carving out a deep place inside him where water might gather, a place where love might grow. He was not afraid of being hollow, waiting only for the wind to blow through him, and he would be music. He did not fear the artist. The art never does.

Once able to keep his head up, he would begin to learn what he could bare (would be constantly learning this). His lungs would grow strong, his legs long. He would go places and breathe often. He would know where his feet were and which way North was, always testing what he could find, whom he could meet, where they could go, and what he could know about them. He would worship women and pull the truth out of men as the sun laid its sweet layer down, he would know its kiss and would be grateful for it. Love. It would be everywhere. The boy would see it, feel it, breathe it in, let it go, kiss, and on those rare and magic moments when he would be kissed in return with the same timbre and tone, music would be made in his veins. "Found." He might say. (That was all).

Though it would not be easy (for whom is it easy?) Think of it—the weight of silence, stillness, the echoing discomforts of the body and mind, the death all around, the oceans boiling, the loud voices of pride and fear and how the flowers would bloom confused in winter, the noise and the rent due, the migraines and the vomiting, the sweat, the heat, the fire and floods. He would know what would have had to die so that he might live. This condition would make him tough to know (but it would also make him worth knowing). It should be said, though, he would feel these things consciously and would not fight them because they made him who he was. He would not be a slave to such feelings, he would remember where they came from and worship that place.

He would ease into warm water and jump into cold.

Be...

He would say, as he tried not to think of how cold it would be, he knew, it was going to be so damn cold.

Here...

As he jumped in his air-filled brace, his heart pacing—feeling for a moment out of control, nothing makes a noise, and then the crash of sudden dark silence, the frozen space, time slowed to a screaming crawl, everything awake, and then in the cold, that rush, that rub, that rough water hug, he'd whisper so quietly to himself with his eyes so tightly shut—

Now.

This is where he wanted to be, always and everywhere.

But instead something entirely different happens, as is often the case when words like would are so generously employed. Through no intentional harm done to the baby, without warning, without reason, just seven days after his birth (which lets be honest, the boy mostly slept and dreamed through, such dreams, you could not imagine), so suddenly, in his mother's arms, he would die. It could not have been avoided and the boy really hated to have the story told in such a way, but he would have wanted you to know something first, something about what had gone on in his small pure life, his glacial stream of sensation, of sleep, the forging place of spirit, the softest skull, he would have wanted you to know about what had happened when he died. Though, it doesn't seem important to the poet as to how or as to why, only to say that in that moment — He walked into it.

He cried too for he had been filled full (no more and no less) in this life. He had known what he had known (and had never presumed to know more), had said what he had said (and had meant every word), had done what he had done (and had done all he could), had felt what he had felt (and had not been afraid), he cried inside for all the magic he'd seen, all the love that he'd felt, he cried, giving it all up to the warm darkness he remembered. It was tragic. It really was. You would have cried too (I promise you), but he knew in the places he most resembled god (somewhere inside of you too) that things had been as they were meant to be. He was thankful to have played (if only for a moment), to have been granted such a gift (he was tired now), was not afraid. He had opened his heart to all things in this life, he would open his heart to this.

2. The Mother

The mother had ambition, but had not yet learned to juggle. She was young, high, and full of her own promises. She would change the world, she would live well and often, and she would raise children worthy of this earth, with hands that did more than demand, rip fabric, burn forests. (these were her promises).

As for the son—she would grow his consciousness like springtime, the way the desert grows color when the sky opens its arms, she would open her arms. She would be his sky. She would raise a paintbrush.

She knew: the baby boy would do even more than worship women and pull the truth out of men. He would work hard, love fiercely, aspire to be his father and wind up something so much more, she knew he would. Because she was going to teach him.

She worked hard for a living. One of those nine to five jobs you never come home from. She cooked dinner over her laptop as she breastfed and then the phone would ring. She was never taught how to juggle, but the young are natural jugglers, they are inclined to throw up more than they can catch. She would challenge her human potential—she was not a human. She was a goddess. A force. A caretaker for all things she threw into the air and for anything on the ground she walked by. She was a guide, she was a compass, she was the wind and she was the rock; and the baby boy knew how lucky he was to be at home in her bosom for he never woke in tears, never at night, in the dark, never in the cold, because he carried her care in his dreams, it was so plain to see. The boy was destined for beautiful dreams.

But she had never been taught how to juggle, and frequently dropped things: her keys, the laundry, stacks of paper, spoons and forks (the things you hold in your hands), the eggs, and most frequently, the phone.

Twice into the toilet.

Though, she never punished herself for it. She never thought to hate her shortcomings, never dwelled in dark places where the things we cannot control go to sulk and smoke cigarettes with the beggars and thieves and the busboys out back — not at night, in the cold, for she knew somewhere, her shortcomings served a purpose. She did not always understand it, but she felt this Purpose in her bones and did not fear The Artist. The art never does. She didn't fret over cracks in the wall and loved her husband for how much he tried.

The husband tried with the wild abandon of a child and with the ferocity of an animal with teeth. She loved him for the way he failed; he was always the last to know it. She knew they would not be rich, would not be wealthy (as we have come to know it), that the mother would cry sometimes, would be afraid, would think, "What do I do now?"

But she knew in the places she most resembled god (somewhere inside of you too) that these were important things to feel. That these feelings would carve the deep throbbing marble she was, chip away at the stone inside her and someday something beautiful (she knew if not something tragic) would be there.

As long as she had her baby boy to hold, as long as her future was but bathing in between her hands, she did not fear The Artist. The art never does.

And though the young woman had never been taught how to juggle she had ambition, she wanted it all, and one day while cooking dinner over her laptop as she breastfed—the phone rang loudly from the wall beside her.

She turned abruptly into the door she had failed to close behind her guiding the boys still molding mind directly into the corner, an honest mistake from a woman thinking a lifetime into the future. Almost as if it were a dance, it was perfect in a way, the door wasn't there, and suddenly it was, and with an unconscious precision, she brought the young boys head into its exposed and intruding edge, quiet and sharp.

And it was suddenly dark. And it was suddenly cold.

3. The Sister

The world was new and they were tired, tangled at the hands and feet. Having thus far never been apart, they were unable to distinguish themselves from one another. Bodies feel like nothing else, are warm like nothing else, fires too hot and dirt too cold, but skin. Skin. They were warm in the crib they shared, their crowns resting gently on one another as they slept the deep sleep of the freshly born. And then one day the mother picked up the boy and just like that he was gone.

The pain weighed heavy in the house. Music did not play. Conversations were not had, just crying from time to time and the toy things untouched. And somewhere, that young girl knew what had happened. The second half of a whole broken, left, unspoken. The girl cried without stopping through the night and into the following week. The cries were pain filled and raw, shards of glass cast into the air, horrible shrieks in the dark.

Sooner than she should have been able to make it out of her crib, she scaled the white cage, doing all she had to in order not to be alone. She crawled to the room where her parents slept looking for something soft and pink to press against, something larger than her to hold her steady. The father, who slept closest to the door, would wake to find her clutching a teddy bear. She looked blue in her waxing, translucent and delicate. He'd open the blanket and she'd crawl into the small space offered her. It was remarkable how quickly she warmed then, how her breathing steadied and her heart calmed, and maybe she giggles now, the way we do when ecstasy grips us, being there, being held, under that blanket and the warm blood, she shutters with delight.

Each night for years she did this, ending up in the family bed, as if she knew something had been taken from her and she was afraid of losing more. She married the parent's purple sheets to her steel skin and she'd smell them, cotton and cool and spacious.

When the girl had grown a bit older, and knew now of the greater dangers and pain of the world, her premonitions grew and the ambiguous fear took shape. If mom and dad came home late from the movies, as was their habit, she was sure they would not come back at all. When the smoke detector beeped, she was sure it was a bomb. Everything impermanent, like it could all go at any moment. She checked every lock twice and she slept with a night light and kept a printer's tray of bad dreams. The girl was already too aware of the inevitable parting, the sudden and inexplicable death that was sure to come. And when she was thirteen she walked in to the house to the dog, seizing on the floor, foaming at its mouth, unconscious. But in that moment the girl was calm. She had been preparing for such a sight. The girl did not possess any special powers, just skin the air could cut from any distance. Her fear was something that clung like bats to her, with teeth and wings and erratic movement. Or maybe it was more wet laundry, cold and heavy, or rotting fruit panicking on its branches, a flightless thing afraid to fall. Dark freckled skin, opal irises, and that hair on fire.

When the girl was four the mother gave birth to a boy. She refused to go see her new brother in the hospital. She couldn't trust what went on there, the coming and going she still remembered in her bones.

When the mother brought home the newborn, the girl looked into the boy's eyes. They were green, or blue, like hers. He looked at her, and she at him. The mother laid the boy in his crib, this one painted a royal purple. At night the girl watched him sleep, listening to his quiet breaths and the world felt calm and gentle.

"Hi little baby. You're my brother, did you know?"

The boy stirred slightly, yawning, bringing a small fist to his face and grazing his own nose, as small as anything, as perfectly soft. He became her confidant, the one person she could go to who really understood, because she explained it all to him and he listened, did not judge, ignore, or dismiss.

"You know when you see a skeleton, and its just sitting there on the chair, or, or, or it might be dancing on the carpet, and it doesn't have eyes but you can see its smiling all scary in the corner at you?"

The baby looked at her with soft eyes, curious, smiling and then laughing at the young sister.

"Yeah, you're right. Kinda silly, huh?"

And things did begin to get better after that. The girl had calmed, had become wise in some way, knowing now the cycle of things, babies die, and babies are born. Though she still struggled to sleep.

In the afternoons she napped. Sometimes on a couch she shared with dad while he watched TV, sometimes on the floor with mom as she did her stretches on the carpet. But when the girl began to stir, in the space between here and there, she'd be gripped with terror, her half opened eyes filled with white panic, whimpering to her feet in a mesmerized terror, she would stumble to the nearest door, often whispering the name of her new baby brother. Her mahogany hair stuck sweat to her flushed cheeks as she staggered to her feet, whimpering through her throat as she went, trying to run from her dreams, her vision of the future, or from the simple world she so painfully woke to.

"Abi, darling, wake up, sweetheart, its okay, honey."

4. (An Interlude, A Fairy Tale, and an Introduction to The Father)

In the beginning there was the lady and the lady made candles and they were like no other. Few people in the land of Lock had met the old woman, and those that had knew her not, the lady, because at first glance it could not be denied she appeared a man and did not speak. Her features were cracked and coarse of course, she had lived a long life, she had picked her scabs and given birth to men in other towns, acts that had given her strength, had taught her what her body could endure. The lady also had a beard, so there was that to suggest that she was a man.

But her eyes were soft like an old dog's and she wore capes and strange hats about town no one quite understood. Her features were largely hidden by her layers, jackets, capes, bracelets and ruby chains, other garments she had collected and she didn't bother bathing or doing the dishes, she did not have time for such things, she was a traveler, her body a vessel, a way to make her transcendence mobile, she practically floated how lightly she did tread.

This is to say she was not a clean woman by the standards of the time. She smelled funny. Not bad funny, but funny like something that's not supposed to be in the oven funny. The way gasoline smells funny, or one's own fart, dissonant and comforting, the acquired taste of a rainstorm olive, its dirt and vinegar. But something hinted deep inside a clearness behind the woman's stench, light behind it all, like a creeping sun on the horizon, behind the crud and crust and salt stains and hair, oh the hair everywhere, she was so hairy, how hairy this woman was deep down, beneath all her layers. But the essence was still all rainwater, it was all glacial lakes, all cooling asphalt, it was all the world she wore and wept. Like a rainy day next to a fire made of puzzle pieces and gasoline.

But we are getting beside the point here. The woman had a beard and what a beard it was.

It was long and thick but not so wiry, it had its curls of course but it was luscious at its core, it just about glowed in its thick black glory and when her beard had grown properly oiled and dusty from the days' labor, and sometimes this would take weeks, months, years she would watch it all gather, all the mess, the salt and dirt, oil and blood that the sun shines on. But when it had grown long enough and thick enough, when the oils were just right and the dust gave it weight just so, she would roll her black beard between her hands, sneezing into them constantly as she did because she had allergies.

You never saw hands move so fast, the air and space melting between them, a cloud of warm dust hugged her tight, light, smooth and dry and her beard would begin to dred into rows of perfectly plump little hair sausages. So satisfying they were to see. They would become hard, solid little things, and using her sharpened thumbnail which she had turned into an absolute razor she would pluck the dreds from her face to handle them gently, examining each one as the newborn it was, paying attention to make each one true cylinders, the black glistening in her palm like a hairy night sky the moon shown back. Then with her eyes closed she'd make her lips wet, licking each one specifically and then massaging them together, back and forth, as a young teen might apply a bubble gum lip gloss. She would then put her thumb and forefinger almost entirely into her mouth and suck, easing the wrinkled appendages from her the dark warm wet sandpaper place. With her moistened digits she would then with tenderness tweeze the very tips of each and every shiny little hair turd candle.

After she had collected enough of them she would venture out of her swamp to spend her evenings strolling the streets and in front of each house in the town of Lock she would place one of her candles with care. Once the candle stood on its own, she would snap her fingers and the little hair sneeze thing would spark and grow slowly into the calmest flame that was ever seen, ever stillness was its name and the town lit up with such a glow that the kids could catch fire flies and beat the rabid dogs at night without wilt or worry or woe. This was a magical place, and the people in the land of Lock loved the lights and they became known as the Lock Lights. The candles burned softly and on still nights they seemed to float there buried in the moss and rocks of the little town of Lock. The smoke danced a veil around the place floating effortless in the atmosphere, its rich scent, full of the sweets and sours of life, drying the wet air. The Lock Lights were regarded as the loveliest in the land. Then one day my dad came flying into the town of Lock and said— "lady, this is absolutely disgusting you can't make candles out of beard hair that's gross go take a shower you filthy woman disgusting. My god."

5. Streusel Cake

My mother used to make a streusel cake for Thanksgiving. To be precise, she usually baked two. The first one having turned out flat or burnt or broken—she'd laugh, run her fingers through her hair. She would try again. My mother was good at that. Trying again.

Once, she left a thermometer in the turkey while it baked beneath the weight of a Thursday afternoon. The thermometer melted (mercury swimming in the gravy). She laughed. (Melted plastic fusing with the dark meat). She cursed, too.

Oh shit. Now what do I do?

Her boyfriend, the Capital Man, makes the stuffing in my father's kitchen. He, having made easy the benefits of my parent's broken peace strewn about the place (an exceptionally clean man), says to my mother:

"You know, you're not supposed to leave the thermometer *in* the turkey. Take it out, Becky, Jesus." He calls her Becky. No one else ever did. (Let's just forget about the thermometer. Historically, it wasn't even there for the whole turkey thing anyway).

My mother always baked a streusel cake for Thanksgiving. An old family recipe, passed down from her grandmother,

> to her mother,

> > to her, my mother.

Every Thanksgiving.

Streusel cake.

And now it's thanksgiving again like it used to
be—because Grandpa moved to Denver this month
after his wife died on the floor of a Los Angeles
retirement home and he started seeing snakes and
men wearing hats like Russian spies in the back yard
that weren't really there. He is a bit medicated. A bit
stiff. A wilted rose frozen in plastic panic. Styrofoam
in a Denver suburb. Close to the family (because
family is forever). He was frail and has only gotten
frailer as I am reminded of the first time I jumped
into his arms and he couldn't hold me either because
I had gotten bigger or he had gotten smaller. No
longer able to put me on his shoulders. Such an act
would certainly kill him now. But we do not worry. He
had been a nice man. It was never really Thanksgiving without him. He gave us all a reason to be here,
he had fought in the war for Christ's sake, he had
made it this far, this man that had known us all when
my mother always baked a streusel cake for Thanksgiving. As her mother did, as her mother's mother
did.

Grandpa sits on the kitchen stool with his
walker at an arm's length, trying to shovel pre-cut
pieces of pie into his mouth with a plastic fork, and
failing. His hands shake, his face melting to the
ground. Someone thinks to help him, but no one
does, uncertain of how the man might take it. He's
got more skin than he needs now. Can't do much on
his own except be grumpy and make clear: I'm not
happy with the current state of affairs.

The grandfather had a birthday that January
quickly approaching and he would die in his bed at
the care facility the day after as if he were waiting for
it, my mother spending her time at his side as he

slept, waking him in the morning to say Dad. Hey Dad. It's your birthday, and to see him smile.

But for now, he'll have a piece of pie.

"Ice cream? Do I want ice cream? God no. I just want the pie, Jesus."

When we hug, his hearing aid screams in my ear a wicked static. He needs to go to the bathroom. Someone thinks to help him, but no one does, uncertain of how the man might take it.

My mother, mixes the cinnamon batter in a bowl and says tender: "Dad, I'm making Grandma Betsy's streusel cake, just like she used to, isn't that nice?"

"What concert date? With who?" he says. His body is failing him. Things do not do what they are supposed to.

"Streusel cake. I'm making streusel cake, Dad."

"Oh Jesus, I don't care. I hate streusel cake."

6. Father and Son

He had been a good lawyer but that had all passed. He had achieved his goals and had made his marks and had done good things for people and had letters from the governor which he did not save and art from all over the world in his home and a cat whom he did not like much (though they seemed to understand each other) who tore up his furniture, not caring at all about the father's protest. But he still brushed the animal's knots out, still assured the solitary creature that he would be fed (though the litter box did suffer some neglect), divorced and trying (and a bit lonely) and maybe a bit too wealthy and old and white, though he can hardly be blamed for such things. He still left the faucet in the bathroom running so the cat could drink out of the gently spilling water in the morning.

The father sat on the couch reading an issue of *The New Yorker* from the second week of September 1993 waiting for his son to return from wherever it was that he had gone. He had read every article in the magazine many times over and did not think twice about reading them again. Nothing particularly interesting happened in 1993—East 33rd Ave saw its bloodiest summer, the new art museum opened, the father was still married and his son was a simpler, if not more involved task. Things were easier, he remembered feeling so young in his middle age.

The man found a familiar comfort from these artifacts of his past. It was as if it were 1993 again and he was sitting on the couch with a stronger gaze, remembering a baby, a boy, a girl, a life, so much still ahead of him. He is not who he once was, he's not who he remembers being. He slumps low in his seat now, embracing the furniture lips, tongue, and all, placing his feet up on the coffee table where, if you looked closely, you'd find evidence of the slow wearing of the painted wood in the shape of two heel sized waning moons, one for each foot the father had resting there in that very spot all these years. The father would sit like this until the day he died (this was sadder than he could have known).

A new pair of glasses that were really not as nice as the father's old pair rested far away on his nose. His lips were pursed as he played with them, a lazy kiss pulling and thumbing gently at his shaven face as he read, squeezing at the soft gobble gobble he'd developed from years spent sitting, reading, holding his breath. He was older than he should have been.

He brings his lashes and lids together seamlessly slight, narrowing his eyes at the natural light; the mole that constantly threatened to fall right into the warm crater of his eye sits on the precipice. This was how the father had learned to read.

The boy enters through the back door soaking wet. With speed he moves through the foyer and into the kitchen, leaving the screen door cracked to the south, the silence broken by his form, the cackle of true worlds colliding and now the birds singing from outside.

The father stirs as the boy enters, putting down his artifact and awakening his posture; going from being alone to being among others, a palpable difference for the man. The father knew how important other people were, of course, though they often wanted things from him that he could not give (simply did not have).

"Where'd you run off to?"

"Shot up to the ditch for a minute."

It was such a comforting thing for the boy, going up there and dunking himself in the water, a shout such that every atom became electric, every hair suspended on end. These waters were the gently churning veins of the valley and the boy was most alive when he bathed in them.

"You look wet," said the father.

"I am wet. Water is wet," said the son.

The boy throws his towel on to the floor with a childish disregard, opening and closing cabinets. You couldn't blame him really, he seemed certain to be looking for something (though he never seemed to find it). The sound of dishes making harsh glass and tile noises fills the room, scraping the ears. Something assuredly clumsy going about some hurried business.

"Yes I know water is we—" the father knew this would get him nowhere. He cracked his magazine as if to return to it, but he would not.

"You better shower soon, we ought to get going." He said, whipping the magazine as if to gain control of it.

"Nervous?" He said.

"Don't know." The son, still searching for something in the other room.

The father takes a deep breath and chuckles this chuckle to himself: *Ha. Unbelievable. The nerve he has to be so short with me.* He tries to ignore his sour sentiments. This was after all, the boy's big night. A prominent woman, one with some worldly powers had planned a poetry recital for the boy. A budding artist, young and full of mistakes as he was, she had ensured it, he was going to read poetry in front of the father's distinguished peers. But it wasn't about the father. It was about the son. The father tried so hard to remember this. The boy would address a room tonight. The night was his. He would speak, and no one else would.

It had been many years since the father had addressed a room or stood at a podium — though he had not forgotten the feeling or the way they looked at you when you had them, the stillness of a room held captive. He remembered: dark wood. Smeared eyes. Walls, words, robes, walls. A box. A cell. A word. A box. Metal detectors and how most courtrooms don't have windows (easy lies of dramatic industry), no transparent fixtures (no glass to be shattered), just the florescent lighting and the witnesses in the room, the tall ceilings, the families there, or not, and the glint of some steel, some metal, hard dark, cupped hands, eyes, cuffs, holster, baton, eyes. A baby cries.

The moment before he stood to offer his client's defense the father could feel the days, years, fortunes hanging in the baking air. He woke and slept for them, sweet confirmations of right and wrong, definition amidst the chaos of truth, justice. He remembered the hands, the meaty crossed arms of officers, the prosecutor's thin wrists, the bound wrists in question, the judge in his cloak, the jurors rubbing their chins, their eyes, and then the gavel. But first the father would speak. He held the day in those moments, could taste it in his mouth, the podium incomplete without him, even now, melting like dark chocolate, he salivated the way animals do, just thinking of it. He had of course grown tired of everything. But he was not oblivious to the fact that his son would stand tonight at his own podium. What would he do with it?

"Exciting don't you think? It's a lot of people coming to see you," the father now just making talk. This is what people who love each other do. They talk. "I like the one you do about being lost in the supermarket."

"No one likes that one but you, dad. I wrote it before I knew anything."

(The boy condemned the father's nostalgia; it just made him sad to think of. He was not impressed by the father's memory, either. The young poet had so many complaints for his father, so many shortcomings to paint beautiful, tragic pictures of).

"How many poems do you think you'll read?"

"I don't know. See how I feel," the boy said with all of his feelings (the father never did see the point of them all).

"I guess you'll see when people start checking their watches," offered the father.

"Nobody wears watches," offered the son.

Then there was space to breathe. To stew. One of those forever silences, each of them making whatever meaning out of the thin, thin air, trying so hard (maybe too hard) to be satisfied with each other.

"Go shower. We should get going."

The tension in the room meant now to deflate.   Details like these are so much easier to digest. Apparently, they are things we can all agree on.

"I'm alright. I jumped in the ditch."

"That's not a shower. That's filthy."

"Oh stop." The boy now standing from his crouched position behind the cabinets.

The father exhales sharply trying to purge himself of his impossible frustration. Huffing and puffing a bit now... *Is it too much to ask him to shower daily? Madness, it really is, you wake up in the morning, and you bathe, that's just what you do, you clean what is dirty, you ready yourself for the world, how could this be unreasonable, how is this where we've ended up. I never thought we would end up here, of all places.*

"There are a lot of people coming to see you tonight, and they really aren't coming to smell what you've been doing all week to look at someone who doesn't care, so please, do us all a favor and—"

Then he saw what pants the boy was planning on wearing. *No. Not those pants.* The tattered khakis with the legs rolled up. Paint scattering the boy's thighs. The knees caked in dirt and oil stains. The pants looked sticky, like if you touched him he might smear. Grease on his lap and a green streak browning on his leg where his fingers might have brushed an aging avocado our perhaps the chili from dinner last night, and it was all too plain to see for the father and his sensibility was now bubbling over. Throwing the magazine onto the table, the father stood.

Oh please, change your damn pants.
"All those nice people, all those nice people out to see you and you don't have the decency to—"
"Dad stop, they're just—"
"Oh Jesus

      how come I'm (he wasn't in control)
   the unreasonable one

Jesus

      how come you can't just

            I can't just

   give a shit what you feel
  there are just

         some things we do
and some things we don't do
      and you can't show up to be in front

of all these
          people
looking
like
a
goddamn…"

Then there would have usually been a roar, a clash of volume, each voice shouting to be heard, no one really able to hear the other but the boy was gone, draped in his ragged style, his father treading water in his wake. Then there is a moment (not an uncommon one) to ponder:

What do I do now? Maybe he cries. Maybe he just goes back to his magazine.

7. Directions on Dealing with the Deceased:

When dealing with death be sure to wear gloves as it has been known to be contagious. If dying persists or spreads, consult a physician (only a physician can declare something dead). After death, place the animal in freezer so as to delay decomposition and prevent its unmistakable smell (you may know, it is quite sour) until burial. You can also call someone to take the body away in a bag.

When burying the deceased, be sure to dig no less than 12 inches deep and no more than 24, any less you might as well feed the poor bastard straight to your dog, any more and the light doesn't get in. But feel free to feed the deceased directly to your dog if this suits you; living things eat dead things all the time, there does not seem to be any substantial difference in the methods of disposal, just depends on who you wish to feed. Do not leave animal in freezer during the holiday season to prevent family encounters with its stiff, withered form. This can be quite startling when looking for Thanksgiving leftovers. If dying persists, consult a physician. Be sure to cry. We must cry when things die, it's how we know they were alive and that we still are. You may also laugh—this is another way of knowing. You can also just look, just feel, just be there with the death, with other people who are there too. Dead things cannot be replaced. Each life roles its own dice. Do the best you can; this is all you can do. If dying persists, consult a physician. He may or may not be able to help you. When something dies, you are allowed to love it so much that it hurts you in places you did not know you had.

Lizards don't kiss. They can only look at you with one eye at a time.

If dying persists, consult a physician.

8. It's All Here

"Have you ever had things you wanted to say?" said the girl who had trouble sleeping. When she did sleep, she dreamed of boldness, of big things, New York City and swing dancing but most days she just hid behind her smile without consequence, you see. It was such a beautiful smile. Those who saw it drowned drunkenly in it and nobody thought to complain for how could you? It was right where it should be. Right there, shining on her face like the waning moon, bright despite how slight it seems. All that's deep and sweet about lips and teeth. But the girl, she did not think it so pretty. Only when she was drunk did she find our enthusiasm for it (nobody found enthusiasm for it like I did).

"A little bit of liquor and a little bit of throttle will get you in a lot of trouble," said the boy with the mohawk as he smiled and thought of his mistakes. He sat like some sort of dethroned king, his knees as far apart as they could be, his arms resting effortlessly on the unoccupied chairs beside him. He welcomed the air onto his lap and took his shirt off, for no other reason than to be closer to the breeze. He seemed to be waiting for the wind to get confident, stick her tongue in his ear, nibble warm and wet, and then whisper something dirty. Tattoos littered his body and if you asked, he had nothing to say about them, "Original Rude Boy" scrawled on his ribs. Smoke danced a veil around him, and he danced too, hidden, in his sea of open doors.

"How do you feel, beneath all those

feelings?" said the poet in his chair, crossing his legs and leaning forward over them to remove a cigarette from his mangled pack, his back arched, his shoulders sunken. Placing the yellow stained skyscraper between his lips, he takes his time setting it ablaze as he had done countless times, far too many for anyone's mother to bare. The poet learned something from the smoke. But ask the doctors, ask the scientists, they'll call the poet crazy for making such a claim.

And how could three people such as these find themselves on the same porch, sitting as they were? Well that is of course quite a question. Almost so that you have to wonder if this was, in fact, even a porch at all or simply where our answers are hidden in the soft light and dust of the magic hour made real; you only need be here, right now, to know it, but don't be expecting much because then again…

It's just a porch.

A house is behind it. The chairs are in no particular order, just where they happen to be. There is just the breeze, just the hardness of their seats, just their fantastic view of a car; these things do not mean much (there are so many damned cars everywhere). There's also a tree. A really big one. Maybe extraordinarily big, but then again, this is not especially special either. It's just a tree and trees are everywhere.

The road is just there and it is wide, the grass is green by its side; cars drive by occasionally but not often and there's a streetlight across the way that bathes the night in amber light giving everything a goddamn golden outline.

Exactly six beer cans are on the table, though it's anyone's guess which ones are empty and which ones aren't (in case you're wondering: the girl had finished hers and had been holding an empty can for a suspicious twelve minutes. The boy with the mohawk was just now showing his friends how to rip his fourth can in two with his teeth. "I'm training to be a vampire," he said, though no one could be sure what that meant. The poet had opened his, taken one sip, set it down, not to have touched it again).

There's an unlit candle and an ashtray on the table though most of the ash is on the ground. It's just a porch (you know what it looks like).

The sun can't be contained here and colors have spilled from its spectrum soaking the skies floating walls in every sinful shade. One thing is certain: it is beautiful. The sun pulls her skirt down over her hips (don't be nervous, I'm not going to hurt you), and she's soft and deep and full as she lies down. Everyone should just lie down. Things have started to sleep; we are all coming down now. People are sitting, talking, thinking. Come sit and listen closely. You're not listening. Listen.

It's all here, on this porch.

There is courage (so much) in the eyes of the girl who woke every morning trying once again to be who she was behind the bars of her body. Two ways the girl was torn: to embrace her cage. To climb her tender backbone like she once climbed trees (just like I did), going up, hand over hand, wrapping herself with care around each vertebra, pulling into the mind's cushioned canopy, warm, though painfully alone, to watch the stars in their dark boundless place.

Or she could shake the bars. Scream help with her smile. She could undress her strong and sweaty companions like someone who wanted out, like someone searching for something, desperate, begging for it, wondering helplessly who had it (for god's sake), so that she might walk free of her feelings, free of her fear, to feel the cold dew kiss her heels. Each morning she had to decide. This or that.

There is confidence in the boy with the mohawk. Also, horrible short term memory. Watch as he picks up his bottle and pulls strong on it. "I'm a good boy, I really am," he says as he swallows and the bottle comes down. "I just ain't a good leash dog. You can't keep me from sniffin' ass, starting fights, running in front of cars, chasing pussy…"

"Yes, we get it, Rat." said the poet. Rat quits his rant and quiets looking towards the departing sun, on his own accord of course and not at the suggestion of anyone, especially not the poet with his sentimental soul, his soft eyes and tired language (aren't we all not just a little sick of these words, all this talking), in fact, Rat acted as if the poet hadn't spoken at all. It was as if he hadn't, actually, for no one had really heard him.

"The spilled spirits of angels, don't it look like?" said Rat in his own way, drinking his own spirits and referring to the sunset. He liked the image of angels in salutation around giant bottles of lush colored drink in the sky, knocking over their glasses with their gestures and their thirst, making such a loud, beautiful mess. As the day grows old, angels grow careless, flipping tables and menacing the clouds, forcing them into chariot shapes to be driven with reckless abandon. The angels of his mind would sit, arms around one another in the wake of the storms they themselves created, swaying with the wind and singing drunkenly at the fading darkness.

To be clear, Rat was no angel. He was simply a man who'd learned to fly.

He bent forward from his recline to a small tin of pipe tobacco he'd stolen from his father. The tobacco had spilled onto the table hours ago and the mound of brown shavings had been getting smaller but spread more all over the place as the night wore on. He did not have a pipe, but instead rolled the sharp shavings into sloppy cigars that he seemed never to be without.

A couple things about pipe tobacco: it's expensive. It packs dense and lasts long and if you don't have many outside expenses, you can succeed in killing yourself long before going broke; the smell of caramelized ashes coating your insides. It is a harsh, black and white affair. There are many ways to think of these particular characteristics of pipe tobacco, but Rat didn't think much of them. He just pinched some of his desire and sprinkled it onto his latter years of decline and coughing, heart disease, cancer. He licked his fingers and took big breaths as the brown veins of the tobacco grew wet, staining his teeth and the tightly wound paper. It all added up to a sweet release as he pulled straight into his lungs. The boy made a strange love with the smoke (it takes someone with serious holes to fill to smoke pipe tobacco like that).

There wasn't much hope for him, anyway. He already had tattoos on his face. But he could charm like the poet would never be able to in a moment with his soft eyes, his tired language. The poet knew this, and would at times go green for it, being a slave to clarity without ever quite being clear. The girl was afraid of charm like Rat's, or at least she didn't understand it and couldn't bring herself to trust it (she wanted to trust it).

It did not much matter to Rat. He was probably going to die soon. Maybe tomorrow. There was just no telling. (This can give a man little care).

"Well," said the girl. "Have you?"

"Have I what, Sweetie?"

She sighed and no one noticed the tragedy (except for me). "Never mind…"

The poet cleared his throat taking in wind as if to make important use of it. "She said, 'have you ever had things that you wanted to say.'"

With careful precision he said it; the way Alex Trebek might put forth an answer or a juror might extend a verdict. He did not like being the formal one, but knew no other way to ensure he would be understood. Not being understood might be worse than death, the poet thought. Though he couldn't be sure. He hadn't yet died.

Never forgetting a good question, he took out a small tattered notebook from his back pocket to write it down with his sloppy left hand. It was the kind of question a poet loves at first, and then quickly envies (though they at times look alike). The question seemed so perfect in fact, almost an answer in itself, that the poet thought for a moment he'd fallen in love with the girl (the moment would pass).

"Mmmm…" He said, long and deep (deep down a lonely little boy, sweating and trying too hard). He made this sound to better soak in the moment (it was very important that people could tell he was soaking in the moment).

She wore a shirt, a gift from an older brother. The tattered lime green garment had faded nametags, the ones worn door to door or at conferences, workshops, the first day of something, moments with too little time for names: "I am: curious" on the front and "I will: listen" on the back. In that moment, the darkness creeping up and down her figure, she looked as though she tasted of root beer milk and oatmeal cookies. If you've never had root beer milk, or oatmeal cookies for that matter, I will tell you now they are delicious.

But the poet knew not how to tell her his feelings. He just smoked his cigarettes. What he did know how to do was smile at her. He knew how to look at her even after she stopped talking, when she thought no one was looking but her, he was looking as well. Well into the realm of impolite, he looked, past what might be appropriate, not bothered with social acceptability; clueless really, straddling the thin line between affection, and, well—

"Could you stop looking at me like that, please?" she asked, sweet as can be. It was harmless, anyway. He thought he was in love. We do such silly things when we think we're in love.

"You don't like people looking at you?"

"Never did me much good."

"Alright then. Where would you like me to look?"

"Well, I don't know. Look at my feet. I have nice feet." She said, kicking her legs straight out like a child to admire her toes as they wiggled in their green polish.

The poet looked at the girl's feet. "I don't think I like it as much."

"Fine." The girl said. "Look wherever you'd like."

He brought his attention back to the girl's face and she shifted her gaze to the ground to draw a flower in the ash with her pointed big toe.

"Well..." The girl said after some time. "Have you?"

The poet thought for a moment. "Doesn't everybody?"

"Well, wait a second, don't you know some people who just say things come on I know tons of people who do."

The poet tried again to think. "What about

you?" he said instead.

"Oh that's enough talk about it I think. I'm trying to ignore it, anyway."

(There was space to breathe as they spoke to one another.)

"Maybe you should try. See what it feels like." Said the poet.

"I know what it would feel like." *It would be wonderful*, the girl thought but did not speak it.

It was just him and her. To the poet, Rat wasn't even there. Which was all the same to Rat. He was busy breaking branches off the trees in the front yard. He said he was collecting firewood and had a point, winters can be damn cold in the Midwest, though collecting firewood in July seemed to anyone watching, well...

Lucky for Rat, no one was.

"So you're afraid of not getting it right?" The poet said.

"It's not about that." she said, her eyes cloaked in a blanket of silk light and lashes. "I don't know how to say it..." And then she said it: "It's like I lost my keys."

They sat together grasping, looking for clearness in the cooling air, feeling alone and together, the wood bowing beneath them.

"If you're worried about it I've got a Slim Jim. Fix you up no problem." There was a moment for everyone to try and make sense of Rat's comment. Rat stumbles from his perch in the tree to bring a branch down on top of him with a wicked crack.

"Good for you Rat."

"Oh yeah Rat? You going to fix me then with your meat stick?"

Rat sits up and looks at the girl, blinking like a liar or someone who's really, quite confused. Then laughter, big loud guffawing breaths crashing about the place, closing his eyes now and throwing his head back. "Shit lady, a Slim Jim's just a crow bar for getting into cars. You said you lost your keys, didn't you?"

"Yeah Rat. I lost my keys."

"Well we're going to fix you right up. Give me fifteen minutes, I'll pop that lock quicker than you can say 'Cut Mustard!'"

"Rat, you don't have t—"

But he was gone. He wouldn't be back. That short-term memory makes a man easily distracted.

To the matter at hand: the poet had so much he wanted the girl to know. He would have laid down right there next to her, memorizing the curves of her incarnation, trying to find his god in her everything. He would have held her tight, told her all the things she needed to hear, climbing in through the cage bars of her body (for he did not have the key) joining her to watch the stars nod across the sky. The dew on his heels had muddied the dust and he just felt tired of dragging it everywhere, all his past caking his soles, he just wanted to go inside. He was weary and just wanted to lie down (everyone should just lie down now).

And maybe they do. Sleeping bags and sweatpants and the poet's heart balancing like a glass of water on the girl's backbone in the ashes on the floor, no longer watching the stars but instead wrapping themselves in the night sky they shared, trading breaths ever so softly into each other's lungs. He kisses her shoulder (trying hard not to be noticed), I'm sure, lying there thinking how lucky he was to be blessed with these moments, and thinking then of all his poetry. He knew what he could give to the girl. They could feel safe (he knew it). They could understand each other (he knew this too). And maybe they do (for nobody "knows" quite like the poets do. They do it with a vengeance).

Then again… more likely they don't. Yes, I do indeed recall it quite differently.

Instead, there was just miles of silence between them as the poet looked down at the girl's feet and could find nothing to say.

(I am the poet and I saw it all).

9. Taco Truck Woes and Secrets

There was a fire on the taco truck I work on today and John, the boss, the man, the rock, didn't blink, he just sat there sweating, feeling his feet pulse and hurt beneath him and the weight of all his fucking tacos, all his early mornings and late nights slow cooked beans too hard, too soft, too salty, too few, five stars and then one and then two and then John will sleep, but only for a moment, only until morning wakes him with sour burn in his eyes at the glowing thread of dawn. He stirs to rub them with the full length of his finger (he will be careless with his treatment) every day, every morning, before the sun and after, every 3pm on a Sunday and now the grill is on fire.

But this is what happens when you cook cows and pigs and chickens, full weights of them over the months, so much dripping out and gathering (you didn't think you got rid of them so easily), it taking so much to make it all and it all goes somewhere. All the trash, the vinyl gloves and empty sour cream containers, all the salt and cheese, the guacamole gone bad, the brisket dried up all of it that had built up and now there is a fire. We notice as the steak, flame kissed, begins to burn and sizzle wet and hot buried in its orange flame (it is hard) and John hardly notices as he stirs the beans (too salty, too soft). The fire, cathartic by its nature releases its energy as we bake in our work, a long dark breath slowly cooking (it grew so slowly), so much pain burning so slowly, so much neglect, so many must do and do not forgets, the cold indifference of time cooking in the blinding smoke. He has totaled two cars this month (the grind stone splitting in two) as I thought the fire would consume us and the whole truck would explode like his kids gone back to Texas because their landlord has kicked them out of their Fort Collins home and John works 14 hour days and looks for another house and now sleeps on a couch a thousand miles away from his family, like his wife's supportive text messages like being his own boss shouting the wind down. He does his hair in the morning too, but not his laundry cause he hasn't the time or place. The fire is so hot now, it's gotten bigger but John hasn't moved, he's just standing there in his CSU Rams shirt, his formless jeans and unmarked black shoes, knife in hand watching the grease bubble and fizz and burn and growl. Foreheads sweat endlessly drowning almost (for real), I am dripping, the truck is small and I am beginning to worry, when will we leave? When will we move (there is so little space to move). The fire is filling the full length of the grill now, and it has spread to a space underneath it (where is the gas?), it is between us and the door, I try cutting chicken and my fingers burn wrapped in their thin vinyl gloves sticking to my sweaty hands (the gloves will drip when I take them off) and they forget their work as my eyes finally stick on the flames and the smoke is stinging but John just stands there breathing watching it bloom up around him with his shoulders unhinged, the fan fights its own losing battle. The crowded burnt air shimmies a dancing chaos through the cracks of our unopened vending window concealing our suffering, our food truck woes and secrets.

I want air and make a move to the door but

have to scoot around John (who hasn't moved by the way) as he stands there stoic as a statue, like David on his marble pedestal and John has ten orders but David will never be forgotten, the people outside aren't thinking (do not forget, there is so much not to forget) between their pitchers of beer, dizzy with them, the decadence of our time and place but it's his calling he is calling your order, your name (tracy, carnitas for phil, dan, kaitlin, red shirt blue shoes head band sunglasses, the distinguishing features, the one with the eyes, the one with the lips, the one with the baby, the one with the booty). John stands at his station, in his tank, the shining armor that it is, even when it burns, even when it sinks, even when it's greasy and the gas doesn't work or the water isn't hot enough or the cheese has melted or the sodas aren't cold, at five in the morning and eleven o'clock at night with the generator growling behind him.

I wrap a bandanna around my face and go back to cutting chicken.

He finally reaches for the fire extinguisher and holds it a long while looking at it, wondering how we can stay open, how he can finish the day and he's had 3 16 hr days in a row so to poison the grill before him seems simple self-mutilation, nails on this food truck cross and chalkboard, this is John ripping his proverbial hair. He takes a breath (I see it) and unloads the substance spraying short bursts, examining the extinguishers effect which is that I can feel it's gut stuff explode into the air as the fire retreats with each spray birthing plumes of what feels like toxic smoke, the burn lung deep, and my lungs burn with it behind my bandanna and I feel for a moment like I might pass out or vomit or both.

John still hasn't moved. He opens the vending window to air out the truck. The man is tired. We are

all tired but nobody is tired like John. We hear a call
from outside the window. It's a customer asking if we
are open. I look at John but he does not look at me.

10. Lost

They say that if you find yourself lost the first thing you must do is sit down.

You must take a deep breath. Take in the trees, or concrete, the stars, feel the rain bounce off your shoulder for a moment, let it all wash over you and just be still. Do not look at your phone. There is nothing for you there, you don't have service; do not check, plus with your luck, the damned thing's probably broken. Let your heart race a little (this is what it feels like to be alive).

They say if you ever find yourself lost the first thing you must do is sit down. Make sure it is a dry place and then maybe close your eyes. Spend a moment (just a moment) listening to what rushes and swells inside of you. Let this sound be a comfort, the turbulence a testament to your power, a reminder that all that you need, you already are. You might then think to follow running water; it being bound to take you somewhere. They say that running water will take you to help. It will take you home.

Of course, that is unless it doesn't.
And it's true, it often won't, if you've crossed a ridge, say, if you've gone too far already, a river can actually take you much further from where you wish to be (and I know, I know, you're wishing so hard now), from here or there, from anywhere, really. Things are getting wild, aren't they? But following what rages in your veins is probably what got you here in the first place. So be wary.

Do not panic. Take a deep breath and say with

strength, with surety: *I am lost.*

This is critical. Do not run, do not go frantic, do not get your socks wet or sweat too much. Do not breathe heavily or rip at your hair, do not whimper, do not cry (this is not the time). Fight your inclination towards denial. You will think to yourself, *if I just go over that next hill. Yes, of course, I've seen that tree; this is certainly the way I came.* You will see visions and they will kiss you in the dark (by now it is dark), leading you stumbling. You will try and break out, the wind blowing between your layers. The moonlight will not strike the ground the same. You will think, *I know I know, home is just there,* a sour sense of panic now crawling up your spine (you are splitting in two, each half now trying to consume the other. You won't know who to believe when you are split in two. Don't worry, I am here, holding you together with tornadoes and blind-folds and children kicking cans). The hair on your neck gives a cold tickle and your body going electric, your chest now feeling both full and as if it might collapse. (this is your amygdala, your body flushed with norepinephrine and cortisol, reason and emotion unsure which is the jockey and which is the horse.)

But you will keep breathing. I promise you will.

I know the way, you'll say.

But allow me. These things cannot be bought or sold. They simply are. Nothing makes them not, not now anyway—

Now that you are lost.

ii. Now and Always

The room mocked her, really. It had never been pretty, as he had kept it (the room, I mean). So much so that the door, ajar, could not open fully without being obstructed by the things on the floor. Clutter. The walls dripped with it. There was never a place to sit.

A woman was there too, in the hallway, looking in. She saw the roses nailed dead to the door, and the water resting in glasses untouched by the bed, three weeks abandoned but still full on the nightstand, which were not the only things in the room if you looked. Any space where one might walk was filled with *things* — shoes, wrinkled shirts, books of all sizes. A blackened banana peel. Cross country ribbons, and a stained band aid — talismans to the places he'd been, the scars he'd gathered, the lost perseverance of a mad painter locked away, never finding what he needed in the piles of things he had. Pens and paper that sighed the crumpled mysteries of every bridge he'd built then burned, everywhere, ashes, lost in his mangled bed sheets. His greasy pants. The paint he'd tried to do wonders with. His notebook scarred, blackened and blued, tanned and softened by moon, sun, and eye, the mind manifesto of this exploding star. It had never been pretty.

But it couldn't be said that the room had not been charming at times, at least for some. Mind you, it had a *stank*. It stuck in the back of your throat and sometimes made it hard to breathe. I mean sometimes you just wanted to vomit, it was so bad, this poor kid, to smell the way he smelled sometimes it must have been aweful to have been that boy, to have been tangled the way he was, bursting at the seams the way he was, all that flowed over left to rot like a fallen tree, like a heap of trash, like a slamming door, like the wind had gone (like giving in after giving so much). The room did smell of that.

But it could not be said that the room's smell did not shout something of life, did not whisper sweet and sour of love, did not tug at your breath with an eagerness—she remembered so many times having the wind pulled out of her in that room. It had not been easy. Being with him. Had at times been soft, but god, so often it was so damn hard. It had never been easy. But it could not be said that he did not have a way with you. That there was not a something inside of him that felt the beginnings and the endings of things, that he rarely talked, but daily weighed his worth in this world, and was heavy, so heavy, he carried so much (it would ultimately break him) this can certainly be said. He *thought* like a blizzard in spring (and this was his curse), but *felt* like dusk on a day worth remembering (this was his blessing, our blessing) and still he would be lost. He loved first and last and in his own order, in his own time and way—always. You couldn't say that he didn't fall short with a vengeance. That for all his lasts and loss and lust and all that he had lost, you couldn't say that he did not know which way North was.

He saw the sky as it was.

You could hear the wind outside. It shook the house, rolling and folding, banging its pots and pans and spicing up the sky with the salt and pepper of the more careless gods—the gods who let the pasta boil over (the gods with loose pokets, empty pockets). It was the stinging spit of the gods who couldn't fly, the gods with cheating wives—the gods without. This was a night for them and for him.

Since the room had been vacated (and it was so suddenly and breathlessly and finally vacated), the woman had been inexplicably struck, in her gut, where the dead end up (and there was company there, remember the dog, remember the baby); she was so strongly and strangely struck (in her gut) with the urge to open all the windows in the house. And so she did. This was big. She still felt she had things to do.

It had been three weeks of emptiness inside the house (and inside the woman too) even as she tried to let everything in. A reminder—there was a storm outside the now opened windows of the house, pulsing like so many arteries inside of her. It was a miracle, this heart, this body, to beat that long, day after day (to endure what it must), the cutting and bruising nature of words and rocks and silence, to break and crack like so many storms so many times (especially for some reason always in spring),

like

the sun shown nowhere at this moment, I assure you, this was all there was, this deafening silence, this ringing in her ears, the wind blowing and nothing else. This was the kind of storm to drown egos in.

Remember—this storm existed both inside as well as outside the house, making it nearly impossible to know where the storm found its origin, where its *eye* was. But I, being where I am, know what is true. It was the woman who owned the eye. She left it in the place you feel thunder and lightning when a storm shakes the ground, and the blowing and the rolling and the falling and the shocking nature of any ordinary storm was employed here—outside the house, which held the woman, that stood like stone outside the door, that guarded the room that had never been pretty. And the storm began to sweat. To breathe and sweat and cry like a strong man cries (the boy was never strong like a man) and laugh like a strong man laughs (he laughed like a child). Water fell now, it can certainly be said.

The woman waited wearing no signs (she was also, at this very moment, swelling in places she wouldn't have been able to describe or point to). She asked no questions, knowing in the places she most resembled god (somewhere inside of you, too), that to know the questions was to know the answers and she had no more questions for anyone. This seemed to give her nothing to say or do. And so she didn't. And as the rain began to fall, she began to weep, the house began to fill. And she knew with certainty that she would drown, she would so quietly drown, as all things that have holes must drown when put to water.

This storm was typical. It could not be said that it was extraordinary, storms have occurred in this nature since the beginning of time. Everywhere the wind blows, every time the gods wake up in a roar there is a woman with the eye of the storm hidden beneath her chest in the place
you feel thunder when a storm shakes the ground.

And just then, unsure of where she might go, the woman went the only place she could have, the only place that would take her at that moment (she knew he would, he always would). And so she ran to him, she opened the door (though the boy had been dead for weeks, blood in the bathroom) and the storm bubbled over, became super, she stepped through it—all that love and death and dirt and devil and what stinks and what makes you free, and what there, having someone to witness this. All of this. And care. And feel that something is gone now that he's not here. (Now that she's not with me). Found, in all of his stank. In all of this storm, all of this wishing and wanting and remembering the past rushing up and down and through her, all that he was and all that he could have been, and them, and all that they could have seen, things were now flying, she was now flying and this—

    This is about now

and here

        and him

            and here

and always.

$$\neq$$